My Principal Lives Next Door!

Written and illustrated by third-grade students of Sanibel Elementary School in Sanibel, Florida: Erika Arnowitz, Karl Canty, Anya Ciesienski, Megan Darbyshire, Geoffrey Goas, William Hennessey, Suzanne Knapp, Caitlin Meyer, Hallie Nachtsheim, Betsy Pavelka, Amanda Reynolds, Benjamin Shuff, and Sonja Smith.

Coordinated by Sanibel Elementary teacher Susie Kinkead. Ms. Kinkead was the 1989-90 "Teacher of the Year" in Lee County, Florida.

Our book is for children everywhere who are learning to believe in themselves. It is also for our teacher, Susie Kinkead, who taught us the importance of cooperation and who helped us understand the value of hard work.

Willowisp Press®

Benjamin James Johnson is my name,
    I live in Hennessey, Tennessee
    —830 Bright Oak Lane,
At Hennessey Elementary
    my best friends are Jeff, Betsy, and Suzanne,
My teacher, Mr. Meyer,
    drives a big red van.

My life is almost perfect,
    and I will tell you why,
I have a dog named Sugar, straight A's
    and I can almost fly,
The only problem is...
    and this is really true,
My principal moved next door to me,
    now what if that happened to you?

You can always tell when my principal
    Mrs. Strictly is around,
Kids are always whispering,
    their eyes point to the ground,
Around Mrs. Strictly you can never yell,
    or jump, or run,
If she ever caught you
    —she'd spoil all your fun.

Putting up with my principal
  is hard enough at school,
But having her live next door to me
  is really not too cool!

When finally I got used to this,
    and things were A-okay,
Something HORRIBLE happened to me
    —a "D" instead of an "A,"
Getting a "D" wasn't really my fault,
    it was those terrible 3's and 4's,
Practicing multiplication facts is always
    a BIG, BAD, BORE!

Megan and Sonja, my sisters, said,
    "Poor Bennie, WE won't tell."
But Mr. Meyer called my Dad,
    You should have heard him yell!

Then...

Steven and Marty and Henry,
    The guys who got "D's" too,
Said, "Listen, Ben, don't worry,
    We've got great advice for you..."

And just as I was about to hear what they
    all had to say,
Mrs. Strictly came on the intercom
    "Benjamin James Johnson...to my
    office...TODAY!"
The hair on my neck, it stood straight up,
    I got goose bumps all over my knees.
Next my teeth started chattering,
    "Oh my garden peas!"

I had no choice, and so at three,
    I went to meet my doom.
I'll tell you this, and it is true,
    I'd rather have cleaned my room.
Mrs. Strictly didn't say a word,
    but took me straight out to her car.
Then she stared at me and growled,
    "We won't be going far!"

I thought we were going to my house,
    but she pulled into eight-thirty-two.
She took me into her den and said,
    "There's something we must do!"
Then from one of her drawers she took
    something
    —something I just couldn't see,
A ruler?...A paddle?...A big brown belt?...
    OH, NO!!!—Those horrible 4's and 3's.

And so we practiced day after day
    until I was really good.
Pass that test, do my best
    —you know, I *knew* I could!
And when it was over, and said, and done
    and I could multiply,
I felt really proud and so I yelled,
    "Whoopie . . . I'm *glad* I TRIED!"

"Ben!" Mrs. Strictly smiled at me,
    "You did it, I knew you could!"
"Remember, learning takes hard work.
    I'm glad you've understood."

And here is something else I learned,
    that I will share with you,
Having your principal live next door
    means having a good friend too.

Kids are Authors™ Award Information

The SBF J. Hilbert Sapp Foundation established the Kids Are Authors™ Competition to recognize young authors and illustrators of children's books. Groups of students from across the United States submit original picture books to the Kids Are Authors™ Competition for judging by a national panel of children's literature professionals.

The time in which schools throughout the United States prepare entries for the Kids Are Authors™ Competition is a time for classes of students to work together on writing projects and a time for teaching professionals to encourage kids to read and write. For more information on the Kids Are Authors™ Competition write to:

SBF Services, Inc.
Kids Are Authors™ Competition
10100 SBF Drive
Pinellas Park, FL 34666

In Canada,
Great Owl Book Fairs, Inc.
257 Finchdene Square, Unit 7
Scarborough, Ontario M1X 1LB9

Previous winners in the Kids Are Authors™ Competition:

1990: *There's a Cricket in the Library* by fifth graders of McKee Elementary School, Oakdale, Pennsylvania.

1989: *The Farmer's Huge Carrot* by the kindergartners of Henry O. Tanner Kindergarten School, West Columbia, Texas.

1988: *Friendship for Three* by fourth graders of Samuel S. Nixon Elementary School, Carnegie, Pennsylvania.

1987: *A Caterpillar's Wish* by first graders of Alexander R. Shepherd School, Washington, D.C.

1986: *Looking for a Rainbow* by kindergartners of Paul Mort Elementary School, Tampa, Florida.

Published by Willowisp Press, Inc.
10100 SBF Drive, Pinellas Park, Florida 34666

Printed in the United States of America

2 4 6 8 10 9 7 5 3 1

ISBN 0-87406-598-4